NITA CLARKE

Timothy
and the
Blanket Fairy

To order additional copies of this book, contact:
Xlibris
844-714-8691
www.Xlibris.com
Orders@Xlibris.com

ISBN: Softcover   978-1-6641-7664-5
        EBook   978-1-6641-7663-8

Print information available on the last page

Rev. date: 05/20/2021

Dedication

To Michael, my Timothy

Not too long ago, in a not too far away place, lived a little boy named Timothy.

Timothy was five-years-old with a cap full of curly, brown hair that sat atop his perfectly round face, brown eyes with plenty of smiles to spare.

Timothy's skin was the color of the chips in the best batch of mom's chocolate chip cookies.

With a big heart full of love that was always ready and eager to please.

Timothy liked to pick out own clothes when it was time to get ready for school.

He liked his teacher, Mrs. Wilson, and always followed all of her rules.

When it was time to go to bed at night
Timothy would hold his blanket tight.
Not so much as blankets go,
But, Oh, how Timothy loved it so.

Just a plain old, light blue blanket that was bound

With silvery, silky stuff that went all around.

Some of the silvery, silky stuff had fallen away

And hung down like thick spaghetti where it had begun to fray.

But he loved his blanket just the way it was,

Even with all of its imperfect flaws.

He'd let the silvery, silky stuff fall down over his head

And twirled it tightly around his fingers until they'd all turn red.

In the morning when he woke up, he would put it between his sheets

And hide it from the blanket fairy where the pillows meet.

As he was falling asleep for the night

He sucked his thumb until the morning light.

Because every morning dad would tell Timothy that there would come a day

When the blanket fairy would come to take his beloved blanket away.

Then Timothy wouldn't need to suck his thumb anymore.

But when that day would be, no one knew for sure.

"But when she comes," mom said, "it'll be at just the right moment.

And you, my big boy, won't feel any disappointment.

Because the blanket fairy will give it to some special little boy

Who will love it, too, and just like you, will bring him so much joy."

And so the day came when Timothy was fast asleep in his bed

That the blanket fairy came and took his blanket, just as mom and dad had said.

"Hurry, Timothy," mom said. "It's time to go to the fair."

Timothy was so excited that he didn't notice that his blanket wasn't there.

He brushed his teeth and washed his face and put on his favorite pants.

He combed his hair and as he was leaving, he stopped to take a glance.

He looked between the sheets and looked where the pillows meet.

It wasn't under his bed nor where he put his feet.

Oh my, he thought, she's come at last to take my blanket away.

To give to some special little boy as mom would always say.

He felt a tear flow down his cheek and wanted to suck his thumb right then.

But he was a big boy now and would never suck it again.

And when he ran out to the car to meet his mom and dad

Timothy realized that this was going to be the best day he'd ever had.

Timothy is a grown man now with a family all of his own.

With a son named "Timmy, Jr." the sweetest little boy he'd ever known.

Timmie Jr. had a cap full of curly brown hair and a face as round as could be,

With big brown eyes and a ready smile, he looked just like Timothy.

One-day mom came home from grandmas with a present she had found.

Wrapped in a great big box with pretty red ribbon tied all around.

When she opened the box Timmie Jr. began to laugh with glee.

Because in the box was a beautiful blanket that once belonged to Timothy.

Just a plain old, light blue blanket that was bound

With silvery, silky stuff that went all the way around.

Some of the silvery, silky stuff that once had fallen away

And hung down like thick spaghetti because it began to fray

Had been sewn by a loving mother so many years ago

For a special little boy that Timothy would one day come to know.

Printed in the United States
by Baker & Taylor Publisher Services